So Few of Me

Peter H. Reynolds

CANDLEWICK PRESS

Leo was a busy lad.

No matter how hard he worked,
there was always more to do.

Maybe making a list would help.

Leo's list of things to do
grew and grew.

"So few of me and so much to do.
If only there were TWO of me."

Just then, there was a
Knock on the door.

Leo opened the door...
and blinked and rubbed his eyes.
It was another HIM!

The new Leo grabbed
the list and said,
"Two of us will get it done."

He was helpful, but found even MORE to do.
A third Leo joined the two.

How about four? Four makes a fantastic team.

But maybe a fifth would be even better.

Still not enough.
A sixth came in to help organize the lot.
After meeting for hours, they decided
they needed a seventh.

With seven Leos, there was
seven times as much work!

Leo sighed and said,
"We'll need eight just to catch our breath."

The eight Leos worked furiously.

Maybe nine Leos would get it done?

No.
Add one more to make ten,
each one busier than the next.

Leo, Leo, Leo, Leo, Leo, Leo, Leo, Leo, Leo,
and Leo paused to review their list.
"Back to work!" nine Leos shouted.

"No time to stop, no time to rest!"
But Leo himself was exhausted.
He slipped away to take a nap.

Leo awoke to nine other Leos staring at him.
"What were you doing?" they demanded.

"I was dreaming," Leo said softly.
"Dreaming was NOT
on the list!" they roared.

Leo smiled, still savoring his dream.
The Leos disappeared one by one.

Leo wondered,
"What if I did less —
but did my BEST?

"Then <u>one</u> Leo is all I need.
Just me, just one ... with time to dream."